P9-BYL-948

# Sylvia Jean, Drama Queen

LISA CAMPBELL ERNST

DUTTON CHILDREN'S BOOKS

DUTTON CHILDREN'S BOOKS
*A division of Penguin Young Readers Group*

Published by the Penguin Group
Penguin Group (USA) Inc., 375 Hudson Street, New York, New York 10014, U.S.A. • Penguin Group (Canada), 10 Alcorn Avenue, Toronto, Ontario, Canada M4V 3B2 (a division of Pearson Penguin Canada Inc.) • Penguin Books Ltd, 80 Strand, London WC2R 0RL, England • Penguin Ireland, 25 St Stephen's Green, Dublin 2, Ireland (a division of Penguin Books Ltd) • Penguin Group (Australia), 250 Camberwell Road, Camberwell, Victoria 3124, Australia (a division of Pearson Australia Group Pty Ltd) • Penguin Books India Pvt Ltd, 11 Community Centre, Panchsheel Park, New Delhi—110 017, India • Penguin Group (NZ), Cnr Airborne and Rosedale Roads, Albany, Auckland 1310, New Zealand (a division of Pearson New Zealand Ltd) • Penguin Books (South Africa) (Pty) Ltd, 24 Sturdee Avenue, Rosebank, Johannesburg 2196, South Africa • Penguin Books Ltd, Registered Offices: 80 Strand, London WC2R 0RL, England



*Library of Congress Cataloging-in-Publication Data*
Ernst, Lisa Campbell.
Sylvia Jean, drama queen/Lisa Campbell Ernst.—1st ed.
p. cm.
Summary: Sylvia Jean has an amazing costume for every occasion, but when a party is announced, with a prize for the best costume, she cannot think of what to wear.
ISBN 0-525-46962-1 (alk. paper)
[1. Costume—Fiction. 2. Identity—Fiction.] I. Title.
PZ7.E7323Sy 2005 [E]—dc22 2004024513

Published in the United States by Dutton Children's Books, a division of Penguin Young Readers Group
345 Hudson Street, New York, New York 10014
www.penguin.com/youngreaders

Designed by Heather Wood with Lisa Campbell Ernst

Manufactured in China • First Edition
10 9 8 7 6 5 4 3 2 1

for
Elizabeth
and
Allison
thanks
to Lee

Sylvia Jean Connelly was a drama queen, with a costume for every occasion. Comic, tragic, or melodramatic, Sylvia Jean lived in a dress-up world.

Sylvia Jean believed there was a perfect outfit for every minute of the day, so she was easy to spot around town.

Nervous about her dentist visit, she dressed as a superhero. "They're brave and have sparkly smiles," she said.

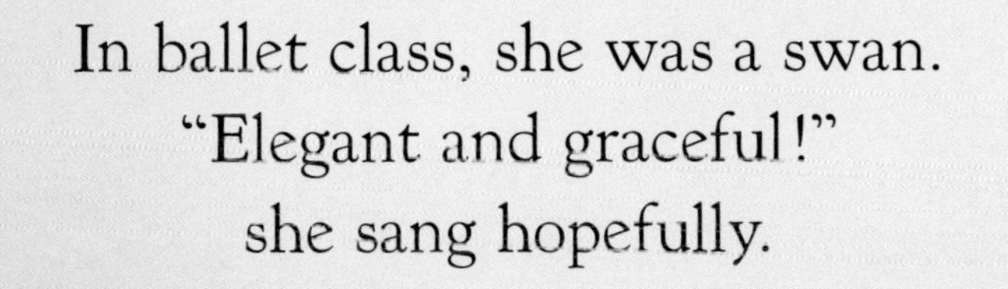

In ballet class, she was a swan.
"Elegant and graceful!"
she sang hopefully.

At the movies, she was a star
and called everyone "Daaaaarling,"
even the popcorn lady.

It was the same at home.

If her father sneezed, she became a hovering nurse. "I'm fine, I promise," he assured her.

If her little brother cried, she became a circus clown to cheer him up.

And when her mother
did yard work, Sylvia Jean
was a bee. "Pollination!" she
shouted, buzzing through the
garden. "Very important!"
Her parents grew
to accept it.

And so did the kids at school. For the science fair, Sylvia Jean was Albert Einstein.

She became the Statue of Liberty to welcome a new student on his first day. "I lift my lamp beside the golden door!" she called out as he walked in.

"Who's the kid in the costume?" he asked.

"Don't worry, you'll get used to her," said her friends.

And for Groundhog Day? Well, you can probably guess what costume Sylvia Jean wore then.

Yes, no matter the season, Sylvia Jean thought the world was her stage.

And that is why Mrs. McCoy at the grocery was so excited on Monday.

"Look!" she gushed. "The announcement has just been posted!" Sylvia Jean and her mother looked.

GRAND PRIZE
given to the best costume!
7:00 P.M.

Mrs. McCoy hugged Sylvia Jean so hard, one of her bananas fell off.

"Congratulations!" she cried. "We just know you'll win!"

"I'll have the best costume ever," agreed Sylvia Jean.

From that minute on, Sylvia Jean could think of nothing else. Posters were hung all over town. Everywhere Sylvia Jean went, friends pointed them out.

"What will you be?" they all wanted to know.

"I haven't decided," she said, "but it will be my best costume ever. You'll never recognize me."

"Of course we will," insisted her friends.

Early the next morning, Sylvia Jean went to the library to do research.

"Ah-ha," she said as she looked at books on all kinds of subjects, from animals to architecture, fairy tales to foreign lands, history to harmonicas.

"Hmm," she murmured. "Well, well, well." She made some notes, did some sketches, and checked out a stack of books.

"Have you decided yet?" asked Mr. Fox, the librarian.

"No," Sylvia Jean said, "but it will be fabulous, and you'll never know it's me."

"But I'd know you anywhere," the librarian said.

"Not this time," promised Sylvia Jean.

FOX

But by Wednesday, Sylvia Jean was feeling nervous. She needed a great idea.

"I've told everyone this will be my best costume ever. It should be something big. Something fabulous. Something unexpected."

An astronaut? She'd already done it. An elephant? Been there. Cinderella? Done that. A cheeseburger, chessboard, fairy, frog, domino, dinosaur? She'd done them all.

"Ohhhhh dear," Sylvia Jean whispered.

On Thursday, Sylvia Jean began to panic. Her mother and father made suggestions, but it only made things worse.

Sylvia Jean hung a "Do Not Disturb" sign on her bedroom door, then disappeared inside.

"I'm not coming out till I've made the perfect costume!" she declared.

Her parents grew worried.

On Friday, the phone kept ringing at the Connelly house.

"No," Sylvia Jean heard her mother say. "I don't know what costume Sylvia Jean will be wearing."

Mr. and Mrs. Connelly left food outside Sylvia Jean's door, but it sat there, uneaten. She lay on her bed, staring up at the ceiling. For the first time in her life, Sylvia Jean was without an idea for a costume.

"Nothing comes to mind," she sobbed, tears rolling down her round cheeks. "Nothing, nothing, nothing."

And then suddenly, Sylvia Jean smiled.

On Saturday night, when Sylvia Jean stepped out of her bedroom to leave for the party, her parents gasped.

"Are you sure you want to go out like that?" her father said.

"Yes, I'm sure," said Sylvia Jean.

"Oh my," her mother said uncertainly.

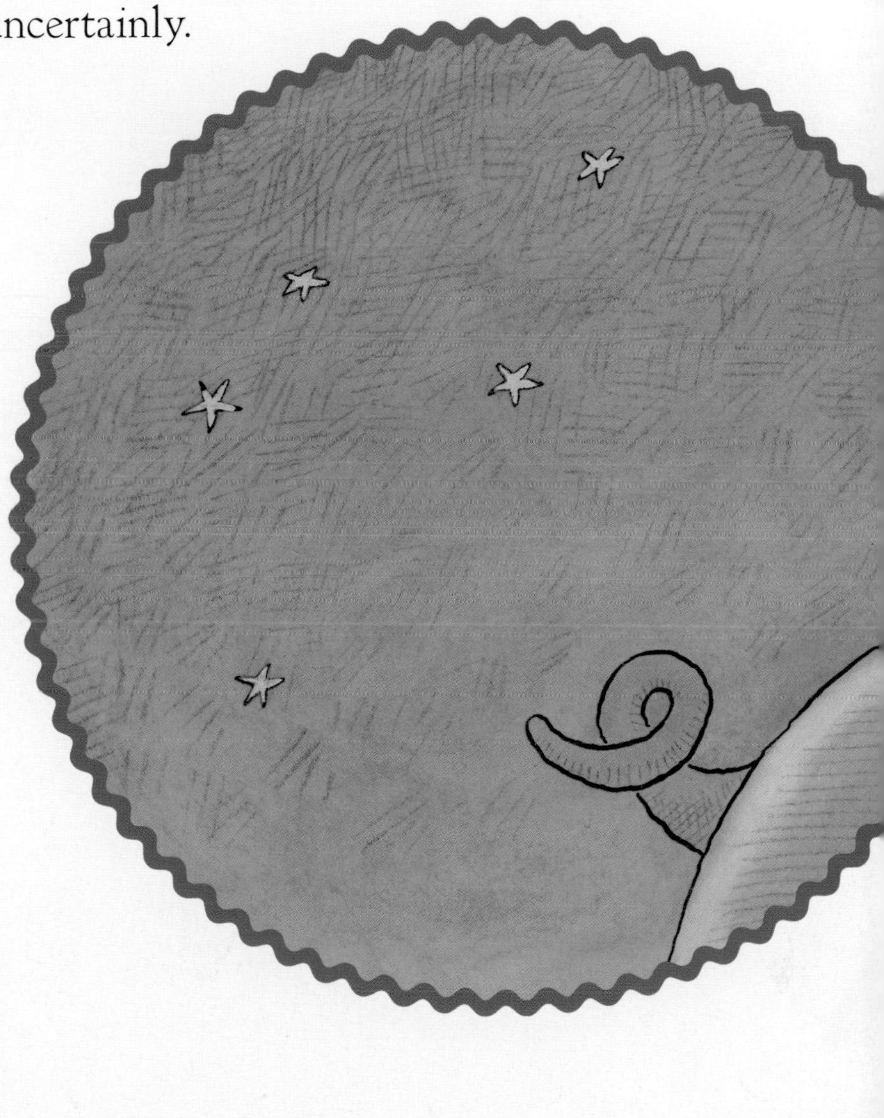

Sylvia Jean was able to slip into the party unnoticed while the owner of Ace's Costume Shop made her welcome speech.

"And now, will the contestants please line up for the judging!" she boomed, and a grand costume parade began. There were flowers, monsters, bunnies, kitchen appliances, and vegetables, as well as an assortment of royalty. There were tubes of toothpaste, hippies, sports heroes, and hula dancers.

Sylvia Jean watched, growing more and more nervous. What would people think? What would people say?

13
K

"Wait," someone called. "You can't start judging—Sylvia Jean's not here yet!"

"Yes, she is," said a small voice. As all eyes turned toward it, the crowd fell silent.

"Who are you?" asked Mr. Fox.

"It's me,
Sylvia Jean," she said.

They all stared at a first-time-ever sight: Sylvia Jean without a costume. The crowd erupted into cries of surprise, then applause. "It's the best disguise we've ever seen!" they shouted.

The celebration that followed was grand: a pencil danced with Robin Hood, an angel danced with a banana, and Sylvia Jean danced with everyone.

The grand prize?
A year's supply of costumes.
"I think I might wear this costume for a while,"
Sylvia Jean said with a sly grin, "but it's nice to
have some new ones ready for
another day."